A book
is a present you can open
again and again.

THIS BOOK BELONGS TO

FROM

Sleeping Beauty

Adapted from a German fairy tale
by the Brothers Grimm

General Editor
Bernice E. Cullinan
New York University

Retold by
Sharon Fear

Illustrated by
Linda Graves

TREASURE TREE™

World Book, Inc.
a Scott Fetzer company

Chicago   London   Sydney   Toronto

Once upon a time—oh, this was long, long ago—there lived a king and queen who wanted a child with all their hearts. But no child came.

Then at long last, when the king and queen had nearly given up hope, the queen gave birth to a lovely daughter. And in the castle, where there was once sadness and longing, there was now joy and laughter.

The king was so delighted with his perfect child that he ordered a huge feast in her honor. Everyone was invited—family and friends, the kings and queens of neighboring lands, and, most important, the Wise Women of the kingdom. "For the child must have their blessing," the queen told the king. And the king wholeheartedly agreed.

As it happened, there were thirteen Wise Women, but the king had only twelve golden plates. He therefore decided not to invite one of the women. "She might feel slighted," said the king to the queen, "if served on just a plain silver dish."

So only twelve Wise Women came to the feast. And late in the evening, they presented their magic gifts to the baby. The first woman gave the child kindness, the second gave her a happy nature, the third gave her wisdom, and so it went, until the women had given her almost everything a person could wish for.

Then just as the twelfth Wise Woman was about to offer her gift, in stormed the thirteenth. Furious at not being invited, she shrieked in a voice trembling with rage: "When the king's daughter is fifteen, she will prick her finger on a spindle and fall down dead!"

The queen gasped in horror. The king's blood ran cold. But the twelfth Wise Woman, who had not yet presented her gift, stepped forward. She knew she could not undo the curse, but she could make it less terrible. "The princess shall not die," she promised. "Instead, she will fall into a deep sleep for a hundred years, at the end of which only a true prince may awaken her. My gift to her is the love of this prince."

$\mathcal{N}$ow the king would do anything to save his precious daughter. The very next day, he sent out an order. "Every spindle in the whole kingdom," he declared, "must be brought to the castle and burned!"

And for a time, all was well. The little princess grew. And as she grew, everyone could see in her the gifts of the Wise Women, for she became kindly, good-natured, and wise.

$\mathcal{B}$ut the time came when the princess turned fifteen. One day, soon after her birthday, she was looking about for something to do. Being a curious girl, the princess began poking about in corners of the castle she had never seen before. At last, she came to a high tower. Climbing the narrow stairs, she found a door with a key in the lock. She turned the key, pushed back the creaky door, and discovered a woman spinning.

"What are you doing?" asked the princess, for she had never seen such a thing before.

"I am spinning," the woman replied.

"Oh, let me try it," said the princess. And no sooner had she reached out than the spindle pricked her finger, and the wound began to bleed.

*I*n less than the time it takes to draw a single breath, the princess sank down onto a little bed and fell into a deep, deep sleep.

And strange to say, the entire court fell asleep with her. The king and queen curled up in slumber right on their thrones. In the stables, horses leaned against their stalls and closed their eyes. The hounds in the courtyard lay down with their tongues hanging out. Pigeons tucked their heads under their wings. Down in the kitchen where the meat was roasting in the fireplace, the flames stopped their dancing, and the meat ceased its sizzling. And the cook, who was just then scolding the kitchen boy for being slow at his work, nodded off right in the middle of a shout.

Even the wind seemed to fall asleep, and not a leaf stirred in the trees.

Then all about the castle there sprang up a thick growth of briers and brambles, a hedge of thorns so high that even the tallest tower of the castle could scarcely be seen, so deep that it choked out the sunlight. Within, all became shadowy and dim.

Over the years, many a prince came to rescue the lovely princess Brier-Rose, for this was the name given to the sleeping beauty. But they were seeking only the fame they would win for her rescue, or the fortune they would no doubt receive from the thankful king. And all were frightened off by the fearful hedge of thorns.

One hundred years later, a young prince traveling through
the kingdom happened to hear a minstrel singing:

In a tower, in a castle,
Hidden by a hedge of thorn,
Princess Brier-Rose is sleeping,
Waiting there to be reborn.
—Waiting for her prince to come.

She is under an enchantment,
Till one hundred years are done,
Sleeping under an enchantment,
Till at last her love is won.
—Waiting for her prince to come.

By a prince, and one prince only,
Can this sad spell be undone.
He, and he alone, can wake her
When one hundred years are done.
—Waiting for her prince to come.
—Tell me, Sir, are you the one?

The young prince's heart ached with pity for the sleeping beauty. "Is this sad tale true?" he asked.

The singer replied yes. "I heard from my father, who heard from his father, who heard from his father that, indeed, the beautiful Brier-Rose is there behind the thorns, forced to sleep for one hundred years, until a true prince arrives."

"Then perhaps I am the one," said the prince. And that very day, he set off to find the princess and release her from her long enchantment.

But when the prince finally arrived at that huge wall of briers and brambles, the thorns began to turn into beautiful flowers. As he came near, the flowers parted, and the prince was able to enter the hedge and go along unharmed as the flowers closed in behind him.

Beyond the hedge, the prince found the castle, and what he saw there he could scarcely believe. All was still, all was silent. In the courtyard, he passed by horses and hounds, pigeons and geese—all asleep!

The prince walked past the slumbering guards and entered the great hall. There slept the king and queen, leaning sweetly against each other.

Still he went on, searching for the sleeping beauty.

He found her in the room at the top of the tower. There she lay on the little bed, as beautiful and as young as the day she had closed her eyes one hundred years before. The prince was so overcome by her loveliness that he bent down and kissed her. And when he had kissed her, she opened her eyes and smiled at him gently. "Tell me, Sir, are you the one?" she asked.

$\mathcal{B}$elow, at that very moment, the king and queen opened their eyes and stretched. A guard straightened his rumpled uniform. Horses and hounds shook themselves. Pigeons lifted their heads out from under their wings, and geese fluffed their feathers.

In the kitchen fireplace, the flames blazed up, and the meat began to hiss and sizzle. And the cook shouted to his helper, "Hurry! How long can it take to chop a potato!"

$\mathcal{M}$eanwhile, in the tower, the young prince and princess were falling in love. Shyly at first, then more freely, they told each other their thoughts, their wishes, their secrets. She told him of the sweet dreams she had had during her long sleep as she had waited for him. He told her that he had been waiting for something too, though he hadn't known what. "But now I know," he said. So they talked for hours and hours and knew they could talk this way forever.

A few days later, when the hedge had withered away and the castle was bathed in sunlight, the prince and princess were married. And people say they lived together happily to the very end of their days.